Swiss Me

by Roger Bonner

illustrations by Edi Barth

Bergli
books

Swiss Me

© 2005 by Roger Bonner
Illustrations © by Edi Barth

Published 2005 by
Bergli Books   Tel.: +41 61 373 27 77
Rümelinsplatz 19 Fax: +41 61 373 27 78
CH-4001 Basel   e-mail: info@bergli.ch
Switzerland   www.bergli.ch

ISBN 3-905252-11-2

For Janet Hawley

Swiss Me

Table of Contents

William Tell Strikes Again

For over a hundred years William Tell has been standing on the rocky pedestal of his monument in the Swiss village of Altdorf, Canton Uri, crossbow slung over his right shoulder, left arm resting on his son. The boy holds his father's hand and looks up at him admiringly while William gazes into the horizon strong and unswerving, like the true hero that he is. But in the past few years William's view has increasingly become blocked by new buildings springing up along the narrow road to Flüelen. More and more coaches come too, disgorging tourists who click away with cameras and drop litter. Someone even stuck bubble gum under his big toe!

He bears all these indignities with proverbial Helvetian patience, never showing his real feelings. Only at night, when the last coach has left and all the citizens of Altdorf are dozing in front of their TVs, does he finally enjoy a moment of peace. He then listens to the gurgling fountain in the square and dreams about future heroic deeds to save his Fatherland.

Early one morning William was roused from these reveries by an empty sensation in his left hand. After a minute of groping about, he lowered his head to see that his son was gone! He stepped down from the pedestal and rubbed his neck, stiff from always looking straight ahead. To his right he saw the *Tell Drogerie* and smiled; his people had not forgotten him. Then a street sweeper came along, dumping bits of refuse into a bin. William strode up to him.

"Have you seen my son, good man?"

"Why, *grüetzi*, Willy," the street sweeper said. "Has the season for the *William Tell Plays* already started?"

"I do not know what you are talking about. Where is my son?"

"What's he look like?"

"Comes to my waist," William said, "has curly hair and wears a. . ."

". . .a skirt," the street sweeper finished.

"It is not a skirt!" William interjected. "It is a tunic."

"Oh, yes," said the street sweeper, "I did see a boy like that. He went this way, towards the bus."

William nodded, swung his crossbow on his shoulder and headed in that direction.

"Where is my son?" he asked the driver, who was just stretching and yawning. "He is about this tall and wears a . . . *tunic.*"

"Oh, you mean Walter?" the driver said. "I took him to Flüelen an hour and seven minutes ago."

"Then take me there."

William sat down and the bus roared off along the narrow road. He looked out the window and saw a sign *Wilhelm Tell Pizzeria Bar Dancing* flash by. Further down the road they bumped past a *Tell Garage,* and when they arrived in Flüelen, the first thing he saw was the *Hotel Tell und Post.* He was brooding over this profane use of his name when the driver turned and said, "Walter caught the boat, over there."

"Thank you, my good man."

He grabbed his crossbow and dodged through the traffic to the other side of the road. The *MS Schiller* was just pulling out from the dock when William arrived. With a great bound he leaped in the air and landed on the deck. All the tourists clapped.

"Ahhh . . . this wonderful show," a Japanese man said to the captain and focused his camera.

"Hi there, Willy," an American woman screeched. "Sign this, will ya?" She thrust a Tell comic book up to his face.

It was a beautiful day and sunlight glinted on the *Urnersee.* The paddlewheels of the *MS Schiller* churned through the water, leaving an undulating wake that spread to the horizon where the peaks of the Alps shimmered white. William's heart beat faster as they went by the *Tellsprung and Chapel.* That was where in a storm he made his last giant leap onto that rocky ledge when he escaped from Gessler's boat, the evil Habsburg sheriff who tried to subjugate his proud people.

"Death to all tyrants!" he said under his breath.

"Have you got a ticket?" The captain stood next to him. "And a license to carry a crossbow?"

"I am William Tell. I do not want a ticket."

"In that case," the captain said, "because it's you I recommend our special 7- or 15-day *Tell-Pass.* It gives you unlimited travel through the whole of central Switzerland on boats, trains and buses for only . . . "

"I am not interested in travelling. I am looking for my son!"

He explained how Walter had disappeared. The captain nodded, scratched his head, and pulled out a cell phone.

"Yes, yes," William heard him say. "A boy about 12 years old wearing a . . . skirt. . . sorry, I mean a tunic. I see . . . good. Thanks, Urs. "

"What has happened to him?" William grabbed the captain by the shirt.

"Calm down, *Herr Tell*," the captain said, loosening William's grip. "The boy was on the *MS Stadt Luzern*. He got off in Lucerne and was last seen skipping towards the train station."

When they steamed into the harbour of Lucerne, William was shocked. What had happened to his beloved city? To the left were hideous buildings that looked like cages; to the right he saw another steamboat, the *MS Wilhelm Tell*, but it had been converted to a restaurant. And everywhere there were hotels and endless traffic. Truly, his fellow countrymen had been enslaved again and must be liberated!

Before the boat could dock, William took another bounding leap onto the landing and strode off to the station. All the tourists clapped. The Japanese crowded to the railing and clicked away with their cameras; the Americans shouted, "Go for it, Willy, go for it"; the Germans sang, "Lebe wohl, Du edler Held"; and the English said, "Jolly good chap, isn't he?"

William paid them no heed. He had a mission and it was about to be fulfilled.

"Where is my son?" he asked a scruffy looking fellow in a leather jacket who was smoking some strange smelling cigarette.

"Hey, man, like you mean the kid in the skirt? Okay . . . okay, man, don't get excited – he went that a way . . . to McDonald's."

At last he would find his son. His chest swelled with pride – the boy was with a McDonald, one of the Highland freedom fighters!

Walter Tell was sitting at the end of the long restaurant, the walls of which were decorated with scenes of Old Lucerne. He had just settled down to a Super Deluxe Big Mac meal with a mega portion of French fries and a giant Coke. As he finished squeezing the last gob of ketchup onto the Big Mac and was raising it dripping to his mouth, a loud twang resounded through the restaurant. An arrow whizzed through the air and shot the Big Mac from between Walter's teeth, pinning it against the wall with a splat.

William loomed above his son and scowled.

"How can you be eating a Habsburger, you traitor!"

"Oh, come on, Pops," Walter said, wiping the ketchup from his face, "cool it. It's not a Habsburger, it's a hamburger."

"I do not care what it is. You are coming back with me!"

Grabbing the boy by the scruff of the neck, he dragged him out of McDonald's, down to the dock and onto the next boat home.

In the pretty village of Altdorf things are as they once were. William Tell is back on his pedestal, crossbow slung over his right shoulder, gazing straight ahead more resolutely than ever. As before, his left arm is over Walter's shoulder, but instead of the boy holding the father's hand, William is gripping the son's hand. And under the boy's right foot, though many attempts have been made to remove it, all unsuccessful, there is, quite unmistakably, a large gleaming skateboard.

'William Tell Strikes Again' won a prize in the Stauffacher English Short Story Contest.

The Quest for the Röstigraben

For the past twenty years I have been hearing stories about the Röstigraben. Rösti, that archetypal German-Swiss pancake made of grated potatoes fried golden crisp, has been attached to "Graben", a word that can mean trench, moat, or ditch. Since 'trench' and 'moat' conjure up images of soldiers or knights doing battle, the more neutral 'ditch' is usually used to describe the ideological and linguistic barrier separating the German-speaking Deutschschweiz from the French-speaking Suisse romande. Statistically this is 65% of the population mumbling a guttural "Grüetzi" against 18% singing a lilting "Bonjour".

But where does this Röstigraben lie? It begins to crack the earth in the Jura Mountains north of Delémont, widening to a cleft that zigzags by Solothurn, splits Biel/Bienne, then, with a few dizzying loops, slices through Fribourg and the Valais. After making a sharp right along the Alps near Brig, it fissures to Zermatt, just missing the Matterhorn, and finally peters out at the Italian border.

The Röstigraben has not always existed. Apparently it is a result of political tensions arising between the German- and the French-speaking Swiss during World War I. Add to this the fact that much of the political and economic power is in the hands of the German-speaking Swiss, and the result is two camps. They are not exactly hostile, but frequent gibes are exchanged. The Romands consider themselves suave and sophisticated, with plenty of ésprit. For them the German-speaking Swiss, or *les Toto*, are slow and plodding, admittedly highly industrious, but lacking in grace and wit. The German-speaking Swiss regard their French-speaking compatriots as having *savoir-faire*, but being unorganised and inefficient, and sometimes falling short of cleanliness is next to godliness.

The Rösti between these two camps is never thicker and greasier than when politics is involved. In a past opinion poll, for example, 58% of the Romands were in favour of joining the EU, while only 28% of the German-speaking Swiss thought that way, much to the chagrin of the former who also view themselves as being more open to Europe and the world. Perhaps this is because the Romands have traditionally been able to identify with France, whereas the German-speaking Swiss have become more insular.

I wanted to explore this Röstigraben, but didn't know where to start, so I asked Johannes, a Swiss friend, where it was most typical.

"Fribourg!" he said spontaneously. "I did my military service there twenty years ago and an old German-speaking friend of mine still lives there."

Then he surprised me by adding, "You know, in Fribourg part of the Röstigraben is the river Saane, as it's called in German, or Sarine in French."

He went on about how the city is divided in an upper and lower part, with French spoken at the top and German at the bottom, how a strange funicular connects these two levels, and about a point on a railway bridge where you could actually "stand" in the middle of the Saane Röstigraben. The more I heard, the more interested I became, and so it transpired that one Saturday morning in early summer, two valiant knights of the Rösti by the name of Roger and Roland (the latter lugging cameras), with the gallant Johannes as guide, and in the company of the fair Lady Janet, all departed from Basel in a battered Ford on their quest for this fabled Röstigraben.

We agreed that the motorway was an unworthy means of travelling to a city in possession of such a treasure. So we wound our way along the country road over the Passwang down to Solothurn, past Murten, the scene of a famous battle where the

Swiss Confederates defeated Charles the Bold of Burgundy and his army in 1476, until a large sign suddenly heralded the approach of our destination.

We were in Röstigraben country. Our Ford groaned every time the road inclined. With a lurch we sputtered by shopping centres interspersed with small farmhouses.

Janet was gazing out of the window when suddenly she shouted, "Look, over there!"

We stopped by a potato field and there, amidst gnarled shoots, we saw the first traces of Rösti. How typically Swiss for it to be stacked in neat little piles. Some bits lay strewn on the side of the field and so, with due respect for local customs, we swept them back into the furrows. Filled with awe, we continued along the road that wound its way through a wood.

"The railway bridge is over there," Johannes said.

Excited at the thought of finally reaching the river Saane, we quickly parked the car and headed for the concrete support of the two-tiered bridge. We climbed up some steep stairs leading to the pedestrian level. The weather had turned gloomy and the first drops of rain spattered on the cement. We felt a rumbling and held on to the railing as a train rushed by on the rails overhead. Below the river looked like melted pewter as it flowed sluggishly from around a bend past the bridge to an open space surrounded by cliffs. We made our way to the centre when Roland grabbed my arm and pointed down to where the railing resembled thick cross hairs. We all stood in awe. This was it – we were smack in the middle of the Graben. He adjusted his camera to where more piles of greasy Rösti glistened and, with a click, recorded the moment for posterity. We were waiting for something extraordinary to happen, for the birds to burst out singing in two languages, but they remained indifferent to these human demarcations. In Fribourg this would be different.

One of the first streets we saw was called "Grand-Rue", an impressive sounding name, but the word "Reichengasse" written underneath immediately levelled it. How could majestic "Rue" change to "Gasse", a lane? Did this epitomise the spirit of the two cultures, the one grandiloquent, the other humble? Until recently the streets had only been in French and it apparently took years of struggle for the names to be included in German. Another street was called "Rue de la Grand-Fontaine". Here one expected Versailles with jets of water spurting in the air, but the German "Alte Brunnengasse" made us think of a well in an old alley.

Traditionally the affluent of Fribourg have always identified themselves with France, in particular with Paris, as a tavern sign "Au Petit Paris" indicated. The bourgeoisie in their noble houses lining the Grand-Rue would look down at the "basse ville", the lower part of the city where the Swiss-German speaking working classes lived. This divide between the two cultures became even more evident in the funicular, the cable car connecting the two levels. When we entered it, a pungent smell made us wrinkle our noses.

"It's run by sewage water," Johannes explained, "that's pumped into a tank under the upper cabin." We heard water rushing into the belly of the funicular and then, with a jolt, it slowly clattered down the steep side, simultaneously pulling up the lower cabin. At the bottom of the hill the smelly water automatically gushed from a pipe into the sewage system. We were left low and dry gazing up at the imposing ramparts of the city. The spires of the cathedral St. Nicolas dominated the skyline of houses packed together as tight as a phalanx. Fribourg is famous for its Catholic university and for two local boys who made it big in the world: the artist, Jean Tinguely, and Jo Siffert, the Formula One champion who grew up in this lower part of the city. As we walked around the small, solid old houses, we thought about the irony that here the usually economically powerful German-speaking Swiss were relegated to the weaker position.

It was about 4 pm and time for us to visit Johannes' old school friend from St.Gallen. We met him just as he was moving into an apartment in a beautiful house in the upper part of Fribourg. By profession, he was a language teacher, but not the usual kind. He gave Swiss-German lessons to French-speaking managers! Even a few years ago this would have been unthinkable. If the Romands learned a language at all, it was High German, and then they only spoke it reluctantly. But now that many of the key positions in companies throughout the Romandie are filled by German-speaking Swiss, the meetings are often held in Schwyzerdüütsch. It therefore has become economically advantageous to understand what the bosses are saying.

"What's it like living in the Röstigraben?" I asked Stefan.

"It's quite exciting," he said. "I find the French-speaking more open and easier to get to know. But when there's any kind of political conflict, people still take sides with their culture."

We were getting hungry and so we asked Stefan if he could recommend a good restaurant that illustrated the bicultural character of Fribourg.

"Yes," he said, "the Gotthard."

When we entered the "Restaurant du Gotthard" on the corner of the rue du Pont-Muré, we were taken aback by the garish interior. Every nook, shelf and cranny of the cavernous room was stuffed with pictures and objects the owner had collected over the years. There were scenes of the Alps with cows and sheep next to paintings of Madonnas and saints. On another wall hung prints of Jean Tinguely. The ceiling lamps were decorated with tiny bright Christmas lights and plastic ivy was wrapped about the balustrades leading to an upper level of the restaurant. We sat at a long wooden table and when the waitress asked us what we would like, we all agreed that it had to be Rösti. The question was whether with eggs, with bacon, with cheese, with onions or garlic, with vegetables, with herbs, with mushrooms?

When she brought us our steaming plates and we began digging into the golden brown contents, we noticed a paradox. Even though Rösti was associated with a division between the two cultures, all around us the French- and German-speaking Swiss were enjoying it with equal relish.

"Yo . . . es isch guet . . . nid wohr . . ."

"Oui . . . c'est bon . . . n'est-ce pas . . ."

If there was a Graben in the Restaurant du Gotthard, then the Rösti was growing out of it and slowly spreading over the tables, until we couldn't tell which side was which any more.

The Little Swissli Story

My Swiss friends just love baby talk. For example, they can't just drink a regular coffee and eat a normal-sized croissant like the rest of us. No, they have to have a *Käffeli* in a *Tässli* with a *Gipfeli, Brötli* or *Weggli* and *e bitzeli bitzeli* butter. Some, of course, must have their *Müesli*. Isn't that nicey?

We men, because we are toughies, go out in the evening to a *Beizli* for *es Bierli* or perhaps even *es Tröpfli Wyy*, but naturally not more than *es Einerli* because a decilitre of wine costs five *Stützli* or more, not to mention a *Cüpli* of Champagne.

The real purpose of my *Gschichtli*, however, is to tell you all about a *Schätzli* I once had by the name of Ruthli. She was a real cutie barbie kind of girlie. I would go down the *Strössli* to her *Hüsli* for a *Bsüechli* with a bouquet of *Blüemli*, knock on her door and say:

"*Schätzli, gisch mer es Schmützli?*"

She would then give me a teeny-weeny, itsy-bitsy kiss and we would sit on a *Bänkli* in her *Gärtli* for a *Stündli*, holding *Händli* while I hoped we would soon go to *Bettli* for you know whatli. But all she did was drink a *Schlückli* mineral water, eat *Leckerli* and watch the *Vögeli* flying around the *Bäumli*. Sometimes we would take the *Drämmli* and go to the *Zolli*. Whenever I tried to get lovey-dovey, Ruthli would say, "*Tschüssli, Schätzli!*" and send me sadly on my *Määgli* home.

Now I'm sickly and cannot stoppy talkie like thisy. Must go to my shrinky doctorli.

*

To form a diminutive in *Schwyzerdüütsch*, just add 'li' to practically any word. The Swiss will love you for it and give you a big *Schmützli!*

Words used in 'The Little Swissli Story':
Käffeli: coffee
Tässli: cup
Gipfeli: croissant
Brötli or *Weggli*: a kind of bun or roll
Bitzeli: a little
Müesli: Birchermuesli
Beizli: a tavern
Bierli: beer
Tröpfli Wyy: A drop of wine

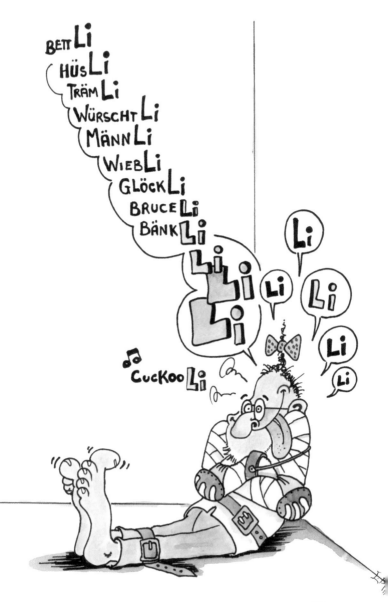

Einerli: a decilitre of wine

Stützli: a Swiss franc

Cüpli: a glass of Champagne

Gschichtli: little story

Schätzli: my little treasure (sweetheart)

Strössli: a street

Hüsli: a house

Bsüechli: a visit

Blüemli: a flower

Schmützli: a kiss

Bänkli: a bench

Gärtli: a garden

Stündli: an hour

Händli: hands

Bettli: bed

Schlückli: a sip

Leckerli: spicey biscuits or cookies, a specialty of Basel, but also made, with regional variations, in other parts of Switzerland, e.g. Zurich and Berne

Vögeli: birds

Bäumli: a tree

Drämmli: tram

Zolli: Zoo

Tschüssli: bye, bye

Wäägli: a way or path

Judgement Day

"You missed at least ten!" she says scrutinizing the blank wall and then, with a flick of the wrist, dabs Moltofill, a sticky plaster concoction, into nail holes the size of fly spots.

"I just focused on the big ones," he retorts, slightly peeved. "Besides, I'm more worried about that crack in the door frame from my exercise bar. What if they see that?!"

"And your oven grill," she says. "It's definitely not gleaming."

"Do you think they'll make me pay for a new one? " he says.

"I don't know," she says, straining to fill another hole within the dirty halo left by a clock. "If I were you I'd be more worried about that chip in the bathroom tile just above the soap holder."

"I've got some yellow enamel paint," he says. "I'll touch it up with a paint brush."

"But it's not the right colour tone," she says.

"It'll be late afternoon when they come," he says with an undertone of dread. "They won't notice it."

"Are you sure?" she says. "But they won't miss that burn in the carpet where one of your friends dropped a cigarette."

"I'll stand on it while I'm talking," he says.

The above scene is not from a psychiatric ward for compulsive neurotics, but from what I call "Judgement Day", or turning over your old apartment to the owner upon moving out.

Nothing in Switzerland fills you with more anxiety than this day. After years of comfortable, blithesome living, all the accumulated neglect comes back with a vengeance because the owner of a building can potentially make you liable for damage you never dreamed existed. It is the time when people join the *Mieterverband*, an organisation protecting the rights of tenants, and make panicky calls on what they should do.

The Mieterverband will calmly advise you that your apartment must be left *Besenrein*, or 'broom clean'. This harmless sounding term conjures up images of fairies flitting about the apartment with magic brooms to the music of "Mary Poppins", but it is fraught with peril. *Besenrein* according to the contract means cleaning the fridge, the oven, the kitchen cupboards, the bathroom and making sure all the rooms are free of dirt, the cellar and attic cleared of junk, and when that's all done you'll still have to pay for the *Endreinigung*, that is the final cleaning at a very high rate of francs per square meter after the painters have finished the renovations for the next tenants!

Then comes that list of damage which can easily add up to hundreds or even thousands of francs, depending on your lifestyle. For example, if you had a cat that loved to whet it claws on the wallpaper, you'll have to pay extra to have the wallpaper replaced. If you are a heavy smoker, you'll be charged for washing down the rooms. Burns, chips, cracks in the wood and windows, scratches in the floor, watermarks from flowerpots, malfunctioning roller blinds, broken taps, missing keys…anything which does not belong to "natural wear and tear" can be added to this list of sins.

"It was already there when I moved in!" may be your desperate plea. But how are you going to prove it? It's your word against theirs.

It's therefore wise to make a detailed list of damage when you first move into a place and have the owner or his agent sign it. Keep a copy in a bank safe and when the time comes wave it triumphantly in front of their noses with a "Ha...it was already there!"

This way you'll avoid what once happened to me when I turned over an apartment dating back to the turn of the century. I had ripped out a hideous old carpet on the porch and found an ancient stain underneath. On my Judgement Day the owner pounced on it with glee and exclaimed ,"What about that!"

"What about it?" I asked unperturbed.

"I want one hundred francs for it."

I think that was the most I ever paid for a spot in my life and I only wish I had framed it for posterity.

See 'Signs and Symbols'

My idea of Hell is to be cooped up in a small office overlooking train tracks, forced for eternity to draw up Swiss Federal Railways timetables. I would be surrounded by atomic clocks mercilessly ticking away and would have to coordinate all the destinations with each other, making sure the trains ran smoothly and were dead on time. But this would not be the end of my agony. Because I had led a dissolute life, meaning not paying taxes and bills on time, I would be saddled with the added punishment of having to create the teeny signs and symbols that are always so maliciously tucked away down at the bottom right-hand corner of timetables.

You know what I mean. After rushing madly to the train station to get a ticket from a new touch screen machine to, say, Vollendingen, you find out there are three such places in the country. On the fourth attempt to type out the word, you finally find that yours is actually called *Vollendingen an der Aare* via Konfikon, but the machine doesn't tell you which platform to take. In a mild panic, you look around for a yellow Departure Board and spot one at the other end of the hall. You knock down several people – a burly alphorn player and a Shanghai businessman – trying to get to that board. Once there, you find that the train for Vollendingen an der Aare leaves at precisely 17.06 from platform 15.

It's now 17.00, so there's just enough time. You're about to dash away from the Departure Board when you notice several itsy-bitsy letters with numbers and abbreviations next to the time, for example: **ICN** (51) 2 3 4 **10** *FA* followed by an ominous all-seeing eye and a glass that look like it's full of wine. The last symbol is easy, meaning you can buy drinks, and you calm down thinking about how you'll soon be leaning back in your seat with a tall can of beer. But what about those other symbols? You get down on your knees and find the *Zeichenerklärung*, the key.

"Let's see...where's my magnifying glass . . . ah...yes. ICN is InterCity-Neigezug . . . what's a Neigezug? Never mind . . . 2 3 4 is only on Tuesdays, Wednesdays and Thursdays. But what does (51) mean? Oh, change trains in Memmenhorn bei Flimsigkorn. . . okay. . . but this blasted '10' says 'See numbers 6 and 7'. Okay...okay don't get nervous. Aha...train runs only on 1 January, 21 May, 1 August, except in leap years. Quick . . . what's today's

date? 21st May . . . and it's a Tuesday – I'm alright! *FA* stands for Family Wagon. . . pity I haven't got a family. Now there's that all-seeing eye, which signifies *Selbstkontrolle.* No problem. I've usually got lots of self-control."

Now it's 17.02 and you veritably fly across the Departures Hall, crashing frontally this time into that man from Shanghai. You pick him up, leaving him to brush the crushed noodles off his jacket, and hop on the escalator that's, as usual, blocked by other travellers.

"Out of my way…I'm in a hurry!"

All the people miraculously move to the right and you arrive breathlessly at the top of the passage-way, and run . . . run . . . past platforms 1, 2, 3, 4, 5, 6, 7, 8, 9, 10, 11 . . . 12 . . . 13 . . . 14 . . . then down some stairs…and you've made it, Platform 15, with thirty seconds to spare. But the platform is empty!

You grab a conductor by the shirt and scream, "Where's the train for Vollendingen an der Aare via Konfikon with a change in Memmenhorn bei Flimsigkorn which only runs on Tuesdays, Wednes-

day, Thursdays on 1 January, 21 May, 1 August, except in leap years…and is only for families?"

The conductor calmly removes your hand from his collar.

"Sorry," he smiles, "but due to construction work your train has been rerouted. It's over there, just pulling out from Platform 1."

Blanca

She's a fabled beauty: large, soulful eyes, pert nose, gorgeous body, if only it weren't for those horns. But then she can't help it – Blanca is a cow!

Any elite member of the genus Bos in Switzerland has a *Melkbarkeitsausweis* – a Certificate of Milkability. Since Blanca belongs to the classic breed of Swiss Brown, her certificate is even gold-edged and her registration number 6145.2028.70 aristocratic. After all, her father, the prodigious stud bull 5078.0488, is legendary among breeders, having sired hundreds of elite calves throughout the world (naturally by artificial insemination). With such a fantastic pedigree, Blanca could put on airs, but she is very much down to earth.

However, being a national symbol adorning the wrappers and labels of dozens of milk products, and being featured in numerous works of art, not to mention all those roles in movies and commercials, can be quite a burden. To find out how Blanca feels about her role as a media star, the *Daily Pail* sent Ueli Wiegenbock for an on-the-spot interview with the famous cow. Ueli met her on a fine summer day at the Hans Bierfeld Farm in Emmenthal amidst flies and photographers swarming about the cowpats.

Ueli: Blanca, could I ask you a few questions?

Blanca (chewing her cud): Excuse me, I've got to hitch up my bell first. Now what do you want to know?

Ueli: How does it feel to be a national symbol?

Blanca: Well, at first it was kind of difficult, but then you gradually grow into it and learn to accept your role as a star. But, you know, deep down I'm just a normal cow.

Ueli: Speaking of cows, how much milk do you actually produce?

Blanca: That depends on my mood – I'm not a machine, you know – but on a good day, I do 11.9 kg.

Ueli (looking at her underside): Your...udder...to put it mildly, is rather gigantic. Is it for real?

Blanca (indignant): Listen, if you're implying something like silicon implants, forget it. My body is 100% genuine!

Ueli: Sorry. It's just that some of you cows have been known to make use of this technique to vamp up your image. Are you happy with your life?

Blanca: Happy, I guess I'm about as happy as one can be, knowing that after a lifetime of hard work one winds up in a hamburger.

Ueli: How many of you are there in this country?

Blanca: Too many, I'd say. But according to the last count we're about 760,000, turning out a staggering four million tonnes of milk per year. Now that's 50% more than the good old cows made in the '50s.

Ueli: That's amazing! How does that rate on a global scale?

Blanca: We're way up there. In terms of productivity, we Swiss can hold our own with any cows in the world!

Ueli: In the past few years, you've been playing an increasingly important role in the arts. I'm thinking of the sculptures exhibited in the streets and galleries around the world. Could you please comment on this new trend?

Blanca: Of course we're flattered that all these artists have 'discovered' us, but that's nothing new. We've been playing a big part in the arts throughout history. In India we're even holy, a status we're still fighting for in this country.

Ueli: How do you see your place in contemporary society?

Blanca: We're simply indispensable. What would the cheese and chocolate industry be without us? And what about tourism? Can you picture the Alps without us cows? And look at the fashion world and how all those designers have been using us. Let's face it, we're icons.

Ueli: What are you future plans?

Blanca: Well, you know, there's a delicious patch of clover over there behind the byre which I'm going to munch as soon as you all leave me alone!

Ueli: Thanks, Blanca, for taking time off from your busy milking and shooting schedule to talk to the *Daily Pail* readers.

Homo Basiliensis

I have lived in Basel for so long that I feel like a *Bebbi*. This is not an illness, but the nickname for the citizens of Basel. Of course, I will never really belong to such an elite caste of humanity because my version of "Baseldytsch" instantly gives me away. I think proper Schwyzerdüütsch is a language that not even the Devil can learn and as soon as I open my mouth, the Bebbis brand me as a 'foreigner', meaning anyone from outside the city. They usually think I come from Wallis or Graubünden. Probably my American drawl makes my dialect sound like I'm from a remote outpost of civilisation.

One of my greatest triumphs in life happened a few years ago in the Canton of Appenzell where, according to popular jokes, all the people are supposed to be short. Anyway, I was wandering about in the village of Trogen when one of the natives walked up to my knees and started a conversation. "*Gäll? Du bisch vo Basel*?" he suddenly asked, "You're from Basel, right?" Imagine my glow of pride. At least to him I was making noises like a *Homo Basiliensis*!

What makes this species so different? The rest of the Swiss would say it's because Baslers are crazy – *die spinne*! It must stem from *Fasnacht*, their annual carnival, which allows them to be "officially mad" for three days and unofficially nuts the rest of the year.

Something else that makes Bebbis different is their satirical irony and appreciation of black humour. Where but in Basel could one find a tram stop marked *Kantonsspital* (Cantonal Hospital) in a street called *Totentanz* (Dance of Death)? Also, in the Old Town there is a *Totengässlein*, the Little Lane of the Dead. I suppose it's where the souls of departed *Fasnächtler* go on drumming and fifing for the rest of eternity.

This black humour was also evident during one of the Museum Nights, when all the museums open their doors till 2 am. Hundreds of Baslers flocked to the Hörnli Cemetery Museum in the former crematorium to admire the exhibition of coffins, crosses, urns and horse-drawn hearses that its founder, Peter Galler, has lovingly collected over the past thirty years. Afterwards, the visitors were treated to coffee and *Totenbeinli*. These "little dead legs" are crunchy cookies which commemorate the Black Plague of 1439 and are filled with whole hazel-nuts – I suppose to represent boils.

Much satirical humour is also aimed at the two countries on Basel's doorstep, Germany and France. The Germans are always teasingly called *Schwoobe* and the French-Alsatians *Waggis*. One

joke illustrates the friendly tension: Why do the *Waggis* have long ears? When they are babies, their fathers pick them up by the ears, point them in the direction of Basel, and say, "Look, that's where you'll work one day."

But this is all in good jest. The Baslers themselves warn you not to take them too seriously. Their humour comes closest to that of the British, with whom they have a great affinity. It is full of understatement and self-irony and often means the opposite of what is said. I remember a work colleague always exclaiming "It's fantastic" whenever I showed him some awful graphic work. For years I thought he had bad taste until I realised he really meant "It's terrible."

So now when a Bebbi tells me it's a beautiful day, I know I'd better get my umbrella.

Tales from the Alsace

Jacqui crosses the border every day to work in Basel and says such things as, *"Bonjour, wie goht's?"* or *"C'est bon – bis speeter,"* – a sure sign that he comes from Alsace. He's short and wiry, but his nose isn't particularly big nor has he wild, orange hair, like a *Waggis*, the Basler Fasnacht figure that represents an Alsacian peasant.

Traditionally there's a sense of friendly rivalry between Alsace and Basel, but the two areas depend on each other: the Alsatians for work and the Baslers for labour in industry and the service sector. Moreover, Baslers appreciate the Alsatian *joie de vivre.* Where else could they eat their *Choucroute Alsacienne, Bächeoffe* and *Flammekuche;* where else sip their *Gewürztraminer* and *Riesling* while munching Münster cheese, sprinkled with caraway seeds, or savour fresh Asparagus with ham? And from where else could they drive home, in a heady *Route des Vins* mood, with a case or two of wine and delicacies tucked under a baby blanket in the back seat of the car, praying not to be caught by the Swiss Border Guards?

Vineyards sweeping the slopes of the Vosges Mountains, the ruins of castles on hills, purple and orange timbered houses with storks nesting on chimneys, villages right out of picture books by *Hansi*, Colmar, the *Petit Venice* of France, Strasbourg with its magnificent Cathedral . . . that's Alsace!

But let's go back to Jacqui. His eyes glitter as he begins to explain to me what it means to be *un Elsässer*.

"We're village people and we stick together. We don't like strangers too much, but we're hospitable. If an Elsässer invites you home for a drink and you don't accept, it's an insult."

"Do you feel more French or German?" I ask.

"Neither one – *mir sin Elsässer*!"

"But you speak two languages, usually at the same time."

"*Oui, aber* we prefer to speak *Elsässerditsch*. We're originally Alemannic, you know, like the Baslers."

Jacqui tells me some of the history of Alsace. Over two thousand years ago, it was settled by the Celts, then came the Alemanni, the Romans, the

Franks and the Holy Roman Empire under Charle-
magne, followed in the Middle Ages by the Hohen-
staufen Emperors, and the Habsburgs. With the
Thirty Years War, eight centuries of Germanic power
came to a close and the Habsburgs were forced to
hand Alsace over to France. But the Germans got it
back again in the Franco-Prussian war of 1871. At
the end of the World War I, however, it was French
again, but not for long. During World War II, Germany, under Hitler, annexed Alsace only to lose it to
France once more in 1945.

"French, then German, back to French, German, French . . . you're a mess!" I say to Jacqui.
"Don't you have an identity complex?"

"Pas de problème! It's the culture that counts
and we still feel closer to Germany, in spite of the war.
We don't like Paris telling us what to do and we resent
them for having tried to take away our dialect. But, *tu
sais,* in some areas there's a change in attitude. A lot
of young people don't want to speak *Elsässerditsch*
anymore. They prefer French and English!"

"So what else makes you typical?" I ask.

"On the negative side, *nous sommes a bitzeli
. . . comment dit on . . .* superstitious . . . *und oi gizig.*"

"You mean, a little bit stingy or thrifty," I offer.

"*C'est ça, aber* we're also honest and deep. It
takes a long time for us to warm up to people, but

when we do, we make friends for life. Not like a Frenchman, where you're *toute suite un copain* and then quickly forgotten."

"How do you feel about Baslers? They often make fun of you, call you a *Waggis* and think of you as farmers selling vegetables at their market."

"We like to tell jokes about them too. For example, 'What's the difference between a nail and a Basler? The nail's got a head . . . ' But basically we like each other. *Zum Byspiil*, like a true Elsässer, I fish and belong to a club in my village. I also have many Basel fishing *copains* and they recently made me an honorary member of their club. Do you know what that means to be made an *Ehrenmitglied* of a Basler club!"

"Jacqui," I interrupt his raptures, "I though you wanted to tell me some tales from the Alsace."

"*Alors*," he laughs. "I have two neighbours in my village, Hans and Pierre. *Un jour* Hans goes out into the backyard and finds his dog standing over a dead rabbit. Pierre raises rabbits and so Hans thinks, '*mon Dieu*, my dog has killed his rabbit!' Hans takes the dead critter into the house, cleans it well and combs the fur nice and fluffy.

Then late at night he sneaks over to Pierre's garden and puts the rabbit back in its warren. A couple of days later, he sees Pierre, who looks sick and pale. '*Was hesch*?' asks Hans, 'you look like you've seen a ghost.' '*Tu sais,*' Pierre answers, *'mi Kinngeli . . .* my rabbit died the other day. So I buried it in the garden. And then yesterday when I went out to the warren, it was back again! It's *Hexerei,* I tell you . . . somebody's putting the evil eye on me.'

"*Nadierlig*, Hans never told Pierre that his dog had dug up the zombie rabbit."

"Is that really true?" I ask.

"*C'est vrai!* And when you come to my place for a drink I'll tell you many more such *histoires. Ech schwörs.*"

51

30 Minutes to More Powerful Schwyzerdüütsch

So, you want to learn Schwyzerdüütsch? This is something you've been resisting for months, even years, and now you've finally succumbed. Your desire to mingle with the natives has become overwhelming. You wake up in the middle of the night moaning *"Grüezi . . . grüezi . . ."* (or *grüetzi* with a 't' if you're in Zurich or *grüessech* if you're in the Berne area, however you prefer to moan). You have this recurrent nightmare that the Swiss are talking about you in their 'Secret Language' and you crave to know what they're saying. Or you have fallen head over heels in love with a Swiss lass or lad and desire to coo sweet Schwyzerdüütsch nothings in your beloved's ear, *"Schäätzli, ich haa di waahnsinnig gäärn!"* (Literally: "Little treasure, I have you insanely like").

Well, forget about ever truly sounding like one of us. Schwyzerdüütsch is such a regional thing with so many subtle differences in pronunciation as to brand you a foreigner the minute you walk out of your neighbourhood. For example: I spent a recent New Year's Eve at Kandersteg in the Bernese Oberland and the next day I asked a friendly-looking local where I could find a bottle bank to get rid of the evidence of too much celebrating. He in turn asked me, "You're from Allschwil, aren't you?" Mind you, he said Allschwil and not Basel where I've been living for more than thirty years! Since I grew up in Los Angeles, California, and learned my "Baseldytsch" when I moved here at the tender age of 21, I was rather proud to have at least made it to a suburb of the city. In Basel my brand of dialect is usually mistaken as coming from some remote valley in Graubünden or Wallis where they chew their words like a cow its cud.

Anyway, your resolution to learn this language is admirable because the Swiss generally prefer to speak dialect rather than High German. The question, however, is which dialect? Broadly speaking, there are three possibilities: *Züritüütsch*, *Bärndütsch,* or *Baseldytsch*. For Zurich you need a permanent throat disease (say kitchen cabinet, *Chuchichäschtli,* 10 times fast); for Berne the speed of molasses in winter . . . *laaaangsaaammmm* . . . ; and for Basel I'd advise you to study the mating call of the rook . . . *jä . . . jä . . . jä . . . jä . . . jääää...*

When making your choice, consider the likeability scale. In one opinion poll, the Swiss selected *Bärndütsch* as their favorite dialect because it sounds *gemütlich*, cozy, while *Züritüütsch* finished last. *Baseldytsch* was about in the middle. Thus your choice is to provoke love, indifference, or dislike.

It's probably best to opt for what the Swiss jokingly call the "Bahnhofbuffet Olten" variety. Olten is a small town about 30 minutes away from everywhere, hence an ideal junction to change trains. It's there – in the Station Restaurant – where all the dialects merge into a mishmash.

If all this sounds complicated, it's still well worth learning some essential phrases and words of the Schwyzerdüütsch nearest you. The Swiss will love you for making the effort, though not if you're German!

Throughout the following brief lesson, I follow *Baseldytsch* spelling based on Rudolf Suter's "Baseldeutsch-Wörterbuch". But bear in mind there is a lot of disagreement regarding the correct spelling of any dialect. In Basel, there are differences between the city and the countryside, and even Gross- and Kleinbasel, which are separated only by the Rhine!

Basic Schwyzerdüütsch

Lesson I: borrowed English words:

Simply by speaking English, you already know a lot of dialect. It's just a matter of using the right words. *Sorry* has practically replaced *Entschuldigung*, which in Baseldytsch is *Exgüsi* (or *Aexgüsi*). You must, however, pronounce it *saawry*, with a long drawl on the first syllable. The same goes for *super,* pronounced *souppa*. Therefore, if someone asks you, *Wie goht's?* (How are you?), answer *super* and you'll be fine. If you ask a Swiss this question, get ready for *Au, i haa Stress!* (Oh, I'm stressed) which you can also use as much as possible. *Cool* (pronounced *koool*) is another handy word, especially among the young. Sprinkle your speech liberally with it to show, well, how *cool* you are, and when leaving say, *bye bye* with a slow accent, and you'll be totally *in*, which is also constantly used. And then there is the all time favourite, *tip-top*. To me this is old fashioned and hardly ever said anymore in colloquial English, but the Swiss make liberal use of it on almost every occasion to confirm a statement or when they want to say something is excellent. For example, "Did you climb up the Matterhorn?" "*Jo, tip-top!*"

Lesson II: Useful Expressions:

Besides the ubiquitous greeting *Grüezi* or *Guete Daag* (with *midenander* added if there is more than one person), there are many other expressions to get you by. If a Swiss engages you in a longer conversation, either nod and smile or look sad, depending on his or her facial expression, and say *Ebbe jo* every now again. This means something like, "Quite so." If the person speaking gets excited and wants affirmation, interject a *jä . . . jä . . . jä . . . jäää!*

Gäll? or *Gället Sie?* is another good expression. It's equal to the German *nicht wahr?* and the French *n'est-ce pas?* Add it to whatever you say and then let the other person take over. For example, *schaffe,* which means to work: *Schaffe, gäll?* Since the Swiss are obsessed with work, just watch how the conversation takes off.

Before eating, always wish everyone *en Guete*, a good appetite. Remember it's not polite to dig in without saying a word. And before drinking a glass of wine or beer, look at each person at your table intensely in the eye and intone *Zum Wohl* (or *Proscht*), *Herr Meier; Zum Wohl, Frau Sarasin,* while clinking your glasses with theirs. If you're *Duuzis,* on first-name terms, say *Zum Wohl, Heidi; Zum Wohl, Willy.*

It's now time to put some of these words and expressions into practice, so here is a short dialogue between you and a Swiss which can be used practically anywhere in the German-speaking part of Switzerland.

You: Grüezi, wie goht's?

Swiss: Au, i haa Stress! (followed by 20 minutes of whining)

You: Ebe jo.

Swiss: Wie goht's Dir?

You: Souppa . . . tip-top. Schaffe, gäll?

Swiss: jä . . . jä . . . jä . . . jäää! (followed by 20 minutes of details).

You: Ebe jo.

Every conversation, and lesson, must sadly come to an end, so *ciao, bye bye, adieu, ade, tschüüüüssli, uff Wiiderluege midenander!*

The King of Swing

The King of Swing – makes me think of the 40s and Benny Goodman bobbing away with his clarinet. But you can swing other things: flags, arms, bodies, yes, *bodies*, though I'm not talking about swinging couples. It's a wonderful word but who would associate it with wrestling? Yet that's exactly what *Schwingen* means in Swiss German, and the *Schwingerkönig* is the King of Wrestling, the number one body slammer in the country.

In the past I had seen swinging matches or *Schwingete* in the news where two hulks wearing shorts over their pants would grapple and grope in a pit of sawdust, locked together like elks in spring, desperately trying to push each other off balance by yanking on the opponent's shorts. Such an encounter usually lasted a few minutes when the one managed to throw the other down and pin his shoulders on the ground. It was kind of boring and not at all like the gaudy spectacles of the World Wrestling Federation I watched as a kid on US television. The likes of a *Blue Bruiser* would be pitted against, " . . . *and in this corner, weighing 350 pounds . . . the Gorgeous Gouger!*" I used to lie on the carpet, munching popcorn, enthralled as these behemoths trounced each other while the fans were yelling, *"Kill him . . . kill him!"* In a *Swiss Schwinget* there will be, typically, such wrestlers as *Schläfli, Urs* against *Bürki, Willy,* and the whole thing is fast and clean.

Anyway, after so many years of being in Helvetia, I thought it was time to go and see a live match, and so one Sunday morning I set off for my first *Schwing-und Aelplerfest.* For days I had been surfing the Internet and saw that these "festivals" were held throughout the Alps from spring to autumn. In one corner of the land there was even a *Meiti Schwinget*, girl wrestling! I resisted the temptation, but this roused fantasies of having a lusty Swiss maid swing me into bed by my underpants.

I arrived in Rigi-Staffel at 10.30 in the morning as the wrestling was, so to speak, in full swing. At one end of a sloping meadow, hundreds of people sat on benches, occasionally clapping and cheering. In the foreground I saw some cowbells suspended from a long horizontal pole next to the Lucerne and Swiss flags.

After getting a ticket, I squeezed through several rows till I reached my seat. The first thing that surprised me was that there were three simultaneous matches in different round pits of sawdust that kind of resembled giant cowpats. I found this confusing because it was hard to concentrate on any one bout and as soon as I had my binoculars focused on some grunting and groaning on the left, a Schwinger would be slammed down on the right. In the end I just stared at the pair in the middle and observed the others from the corner of each eye. Three referees dressed in the traditional garb of a *Senne*, an Alpine herdsman, were present to make sure the yanking was done according to the rules.

The scene reminded me of ancient Rome and gladiators, but the origin of *Hoselupf*, or pants lifting as Schwingen is also called in the vernacular, goes back to the Middle Ages and Alpine games. In the 16th and 17th centuries, these matches were even forbidden. Why I can't imagine. Perhaps the Church considered them too sexy.

Ultimately the ban was lifted and Schwingen became official in 1855 when the wrestlers were allowed to participate in the *Eidgenössische Turnfest*, the Federal Gymnastics Festival. Ever since this sport has become as much a part of Swiss popular culture as eating fondue.

Back in the arena, I was being enveloped in a cloud of smoke emitted by dozens of spectators puffing on long, twisted Brissago cigars. I noticed a preponderance of baseball caps and flowery Hawaiian shirts draped over bulging girths. Then there was suddenly music. Behind the pits members of a *Ländlerkapelle* were playing ditties on a bass fiddle, two accordions, and a clarinet while up front the Schwingers swayed about, looking as if they were dancing a crunching waltz.

"Heiliger Bimbam!" exclaimed a man next to me, which means something like "Holy Cow".

The crowd whooped and surged. Obviously one of the local boys had won. I didn't know much about the rules of Schwingen but the best wrestlers of each canton compete against each other and the crème de la crème, who gets a live bull as first prize, is crowned *Schwingerkönig*. Such a champion attains the status of *Volksheld*, a hero of the people, and is celebrated all over the country.

The Ländlerkapelle had stopped playing and the crowd began to disperse. It was time for the lunch break. According to the programme, the matches would continue all afternoon. Since this was also an *Aelplerfest*, I decided to look around. In another meadow some *Fahnenschwingen*, flag swinging, was going on, accompanied by yodelling and Alphorn blowing. One thing I noticed was the lack of obvious tourists. This festival seemed to be a living tradition for and by the people and not organized by the local tourist board.

I wandered down to the *Schwingerhaus* where I heard there was *Steinstosse,* stone tossing. Now these are not the kind of pebbles you flip into ponds; they are massive chunks of granite that can weigh up to 83.5 kilos, such as the famous *Unspunnenstein.* The Rigi-Stein was a 'mere' 50 kilos. When I arrived a bearded giant wearing a red T-shirt had just thrown the stone in the air. Immediately a man with a measuring tape rushed to where it had landed in a minor crater.

"Two metres thirty!" he shouted while another man recorded the distance in a ledger.

"Is that good?" I asked one of the onlookers.

"The best so far is three metres and sixty centimetres," he answered, sizing me up. "Wanna try it?"

I discretely declined.

Another bearded giant lumbered ahead and, with a painful grunt, heaved the stone onto his right shoulder. He agonizingly raised it in the air, his biceps bulging, his knees quivering. As he was about to toss it forwards, a bright little butterfly flitted through the air and alighted ever so gently on the edge of the stone. The giant ground his teeth and began to teeter

and totter until he lost his balance and fell backwards with a mighty crash. Visibly startled, the butterfly hastily flew off towards the horizon. I too thought it was appropriate to leave and headed towards what sounded like cow bells clanging.

It was an *Alpaufzug*, a kind of procession where the cattle are taken to their summer pastures, led by flag bearers, with yodellers close behind filling the air with their ululations. Then a herd of cows appeared, single file, horns garnished with wreaths of flowers, followed by milkmaids and cheese-makers totting buckets and butter churns. Boys came skipping along clad as herdsmen with goats in tow. More men trudged along wielding Alphorns like bazookas. To crown it all, a hefty swain brought up the rear with a wooden cradle strapped to his shoulders. Inside was a real baby tied down with a belt!

At the sight of all this I could feel my breast swelling with pride that in my veins there also flowed the blood of a true *Eidgenosse*, but before these patriotic stirrings got the best of me, I quickly returned to the Lowlands where the atmosphere is less giddy.

Fiery Fasnacht

Did you know that Switzerland is a fireman's nightmare? If you have a hard time believing this, then go to *Chienbäse* in Liestal on the Sunday evening before the Basler Fasnacht, but don't forget to wear asbestos underpants because you'll be in for the 'hottest' night of your life.

Chienbäse are torches made of resinous pine-wood that symbolise brooms (Bäse or Besen) for sweeping out the winter. Lusty young men tradition-ally carry them through the main street of Liestal, and you have to be pretty lusty to heave up to 70 kilos of burning logs on your shoulders. However, in the past few years lusty young maids have also joined this male domain, and even children, with lighter loads of course. The custom is ancient, going back to the Celts, and was banned after the Reformation for be-ing too 'heathen', yet it could never entirely be

stamped out. It was reinstated in 1800 by youth or-
ganisations that collected wood to burn before Fasnacht. By the second half of the 19th century it had become a children's festival, with boys and girls carry-
ing lamps and young men bearing torches. In the
1930s, foolhardy young men began to fill cauldrons
with wood which they placed on iron carts to be
pulled blazing through the city.

This was too much for the authorities and they
squelched the activities. But the custom was resur-
rected in 1961 during the *Eidgenössische Trachten-
fest,* the Swiss Festival of Folk Costumes, and it was
such a success that it became an institution.

Although Basel is a mere 20 minutes away
from Liestal, most Baslers have never seen *Chienbäse*. Perhaps this is because such a Fiery Fasnacht
is a rival to its own great event and takes place the
evening before *Morgestraich* when everyone is busy
preparing to be up and in town at the stroke of 4 am.

I too had heard about *Chienbäse* for years and
never went. It was American friends who finally con-
vinced me to go with a "Wow, it was just terrific!"
They warned me to wear old clothes and to be there
early enough for a 'safe place'. So I headed for
Liestal on the Sunday evening with a Swiss friend.
We arrived at about 6.30 pm and had to push our way
through the crowds to the town centre. The best

place to be, the Americans had said, is near the main tower gate – in the back row. However, by the time we got there the street was so packed that we had to stand in front. But what could possibly go wrong? Every twenty metres or so a sturdy fireman was posted, gripping a large water hose. We would just get heated up a bit and the whole thing would be over in less than an hour . . . we thought.

At 7.15 pm the city lights went out. For the next quarter of an hour, many fifers and drummers marched by in bright costumes, just like at the Basler Fasnacht. This was, so to speak, a 'warming-up' for in the distance I could see traces of glimmering torches wending their way downhill towards the main gate. Then, for the next twenty minutes, one man after another (with an occasional woman and child) trudged past us, bearing the huge *Chienbäse* on their shoulders, the burning wood sizzling and crackling just inches away from their heads. They wore bizarre metal helmets – sieves, buckets and such – and fireproof mantles, but still I could not understand how they could take all that heat.

For us spectators it wasn't that bad and I was beginning to wonder what all the fuss had been about. If a brand dropped on the ground, one of the firemen would immediately douse it with a deft squirt of his hose. But then they started spraying the roofs of buildings and the walls of the gate. This made me suspect that we were in for more than just a romantic campfire. As I looked through the gate, I could make out what looked like a burning house rolling towards us. When this conflagration reached the gate, the crowds surged back and hurrahed.

Six men, dragging long chains attached to an iron wagon, came through the archway like inmates from hell. A few metres behind them, giant hands of fire were clawing up the sides of the tower. Now these damned souls were plodding towards us!

The people started covering their heads with caps and hoods while others crouched. We just stood there naively until the wagon was in front of us. Then a shooting flame and blast of heat hit me, instantly making me feel at one with St. Joan of Arc at the stake. I ducked and fumbled for that precious little hood tucked away in the collar of my jacket.

The next wagon followed close behind, so we braced ourselves again. Since this was our first *Chienbäse*, we failed to notice the significance of streetlamps hanging overhead. The spot we had so haphazardly chosen was free of such lamps and hence an ideal place for the wagons to linger, and the following ones lingered and lingered till I felt done on one side.

The 'scorching parade' went on like that for over an hour! I never yearned so much for rain, for a nice cloudburst to dump tons of water right over downtown Liestal, but the sky remained cruelly clear. Finally, the last of those lusty men and women passed by with their smouldering torches, and the whole thing was over.

The crowds began to disperse. We walked back to the train station, cinders crunching underfoot, coughing and hacking along with the other peo-

ple like chain smokers in the morning. My glasses were covered with a thick layer of soot. As a matter of fact soot was everywhere: in my hair, my nose, my beard, even in my underwear. Yet in spite of all the discomfort, I felt that I had witnessed one of the most spectacular events of my life. That Sunday evening changed me forever. I'm now seriously thinking of making a hot career move and going into the fire insurance business . . .

I *must* go back again to Liestal to *Chienbäse!*

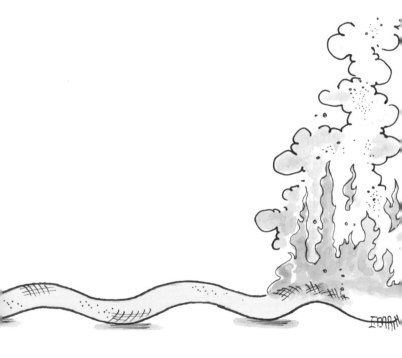

Planned Spontaneity

I'm tired of hearing that the Swiss aren't spontaneous, that you can't just phone them and say, "What about a drink tonight?" or "Let's go to the movies", without them groaning at the other end and giving you a plethora of excuses, ranging from, "I'm sorry, it's my laundry day" to "A friend of mine is dropping in – we arranged it a year ago", or even "I have to be in bed by 10 because I'm working tomorrow!"

It's not true. The Swiss are a very spontaneous people, but they must plan it. Now you may think that 'planned spontaneity' is a contradiction in terms, but I disagree. Just think about all the spontaneous things in life you attempted which flopped, all those unexpected visits to friends who weren't at home (or had turned off the lights and were hiding when they saw you coming); all the impulsive ideas like "Let's go swimming naked in the lake", and you were arrested by the police; the on-the-spur-of-the moment

actions such as singing and dancing in a bank, after which you were quietly taken away to some clinic on the edge of town.

'Planned spontaneity' does away with all the unpleasant, unexpected vicissitudes of daily life which the Swiss so fear and abhor. Planned spontaneity eliminates the risk of failure and guarantees a maximum of fun where you can always let your hair down.

But that's enough of theory. Let's see how 'planned spontaneity' works in practice. I recently talked to a Greek colleague, Georgios, whose eyes lit up as I explained this novel concept. Now no one will deny that the Greeks aren't spontaneous, or the Italians, not to mention the South Americans who veritably exude spontaneity and will drop in on you at 3 am in the morning just to say "Hello".

Georgios immediately tested 'planned spontaneity' by going to Swiss friends and casually, unobtrusively hinting at a party that might take place at his home in two weeks or so, perhaps on a Friday evening, say the 15 of August at roughly around 8 pm. And if he was so inclined that evening, he might possibly rustle up something to eat. He was quick to assure his friends that this date was nothing definite. Therefore they should on no account check their diaries and come back with an excuse that they couldn't make it that evening because the washing machine was going to break down and flood the laundry room. He told me that he would never forget the expression of relief on their faces and how they enthusiastically said they may, on a whim, possibly pop in that evening, asking, after a moment's pause, "What should we bring?"

The party was a huge success. On Friday, 15 August, at 8 pm sharp, a dozen people rang Georgios' doorbell, crying out, "Surprise. . . surprise, we thought we would visit you unexpectedly!" Georgios feigned mild shock, saying, "Oh, it's a good thing I didn't go out. Well, as long as you're here, please come in. I just happened to have slapped together a gallon of *tzatziki* as a starter, followed by my wonderful *fasolada* bean soup, with, of course, a succulent *mousaka* as the main course."

The ouzo flowed late into the night as all the Swiss danced on the table and smashed his dishes on the living room floor. "They loved it so much," he told me with an undertone of dread in his voice, "that they're already planning the next spontaneous party."

Encouraged by this positive outcome, I decided to apply my concept to other areas of Swiss life, for example, punctuality. I'm sure most of you have given up hope of ever beating the Swiss at this game. No matter how hard you try, they will always be first for any appointment or date and if this is increasingly making you feel guilty and inadequate, then 'planned lateness' is the thing for you!

This revolutionary idea occurred to me one day when I phoned my Swiss printer, with whom I had been dealing for years, and asked him to come by the office at 14.00 to pick up a book project. He told me that he couldn't make it quite that early, but 14.15 would be suitable. I said this was no problem and that I would be waiting. He arrived promptly at 14.15 and apologized for being late. I reminded him that it was fine because we had planned the lateness. He thought for a moment and smiled.

"You're right, I was late on time!"

So whenever you are invited to a Swiss home and they want you to be there at 19.30, tell them you'll be late, that you'll come at 19.45, and see how it pleases them because the lateness is planned.

I tried this out on a friend who has been re-proaching me for my lack of punctuality. We meet once a week at 17.30 to have a drink and I always ar-rive a minute or two late. I told him that I would be five minutes late the following Monday and guess what? It worked! For the first time we both turned up at ex-actly 17.35. He was so excited that he now plans lateness with all his friends and business associates. And they in turn are using it too, and their friends, and the friends of the friends of the friends . . . to such an extent that 'planned lateness' is slowly conquering the country.

I've heard that the Federal Railway, a bastion of punctuality, is starting to plan lateness just to prove they have a human side.

When Do You Become Swiss?

In the late sixties I returned to the German-speaking part of Switzerland, a stranger in my own country. Born in Geneva, I left with my family when six years old to grow up in Los Angeles. I spoke English with a Southern Californian drawl and smiled a lot, until one day at a party a young woman came up to me and asked, "Why are you smiling and laughing all the time?" That's when I began to feel something was wrong. It happened again another time when I nonchalantly asked some Swiss friends who had bought a new car, "How much did you pay for it?", or when the conversation turned to work, "How much do you earn?", and saw them stiffen and quickly change the subject.

From then on I avoided topics concerning money and put a brake on effusive smiling. My lax attitude towards time also changed. I stopped coming late to parties and appointments and didn't make phone calls after 9 pm, and I never, ever again dropped in on people unannounced. I learned to shake hands with old friends whenever I met them and dutifully kissed women three times on the cheek, right, left, right. Now that was pleasant. And so it went on – I was gradually transmogrifying. The technical term for this is "adapting to the new culture", but I prefer to think of it as being taken over by some alien force like "The Invasion of the Body Snatchers", a classic science fiction movie of the 50s. Step by step, the insidious process took its course until I was a perfect Swiss.

To help people who come to live and work in Switzerland recognize such a transformation of their personalities, I have compiled the following fifty signs of altered behaviour. Obviously it was impossible to include the whole world, so if I've missed your country, please don't feel offended. Just send me your own personal favourite and you'll get a small Swiss flag as a reward.

You know you have become a Swiss when:

1. You leave parties before midnight.
2. You don't take a bath or flush the toilet after 10 pm because it's against the apartment rules.
3. You begin work before 8 am and leave by 5 pm.

4. You eat a full meal for lunch at noon sharp.

5. You have Birchermüesli for supper.

6. You say "Grüetzi" to perfect strangers when rambling through woods and fields.

7. You think it's a good thing that shops close at 6.30 pm and are not open on Sundays.

8. You say "Grüetzi" to people in lifts and then stare at their feet till you arrive at your floor.

9. If you're British, you elbow your way into trams and buses and block escalators.

10. If you're Australian you start drinking beer out of a glass.

11. If you're Italian you don't sing in the streets anymore and find your home country chaotic and noisy.

12. If you're from Spain, you eat supper at 6 pm.

13. If you're German, you stop saying "Fränkli" for a franc, thinking that's correct *Schwyzerdüütsch*. The right word ist *Stutz* or *Stützli*.

14. You take laxatives in Spring for *ein Blutreinigungskur*, a blood-cleaning cure.

15. You become irritable and suffer from headaches during the *Föhn*.

16. You bicker with tenants in your building because they didn't clean the washing machine properly and you get into a fight with them if they use the laundry room on your scheduled day.

17. If you're Japanese you prefer *Rösti* and *Bratwurst* to *Sushi,* and leave work before your boss.

18. If you're South American you come only one hour late to parties.

19. If you're from India you prefer to watch soccer instead of cricket.

20. You're suspicious of new neighbours who haven't put up any curtains.

21. You yodel in the shower.

22. You think it's OK that the cantons have school holidays at different times.

23. You watch Jass programmes on TV and actually want to learn how to play this card game.
24. If you're from the U.S., you wish people "en Guete" or "bon appetit" before digging in and you use a knife and fork at the same time. You also think air conditioning is unhealthy.
25. You can tell which part of the country people come from by their dialect, whether they are from Zurich, Berne, Basel, St. Gallen, and even from an outside village.

26. You know bus and tram schedules by heart.
27. If you're Canadian, you find it cosy to live in small, cramped spaces and you think Swiss snow is warmer.
28. You understand train timetables and what all the little symbols mean.
29. If you're French you find Swiss wines good.
30. You memorize the names and altitudes of mountain peaks.
31. You plan dates and appointments weeks in advance.
32. You give up sex on your laundry day.
33. If you're male, you always carry a Swiss Army knife in your pocket.
34. In restaurants you ask for sparkling mineral water and not tap water and are ready to pay five or more francs for it.
35. You clean up during parties and expect the guests to help with the washing up.
36. You only trust Swiss produce.
37. You panic when unemployment rises above 4%.
38. You think mothers should stay home until their children are 21.
39. You understand the difference between Swiss political parties, for example SVP, FDP, CVP and SP.

40. If you're Greek you plan spontaneous parties to which nobody comes.
41. You think it's democratic to have seven heads of government.
42. If you're from Turkey, you sort your garbage and neatly bundle up old newspapers.
43. You complain all the time about how stressed you are and how the work is too much.
44. You won't eat fondue or raclett in summer.
45. You think draughts of air cause all kinds of horrible illnesses from stiff necks to pneumonia.
46. You worry if you have enough insurances.
47. You think it's OK for Swiss soldiers to keep submachine guns and live ammunition at home.
48. You sprinkle Aromat on your food.
49. You organise apéros for everything and expect others to do likewise.
50. And finally, you don't think that I'm funny.

If you have regularly been doing three or more of these things, then you're definitely being taken over. Don't panic and fight against it. Remember, Switzerland may be small, but it's bigger than you!

The Bottle Bank

It was at the beginning of January, that time when everyone is recuperating from the excesses of Christmas and New Year's parties, when I decided to get rid of all my empty wine and Champagne bottles. Nothing like beginning the year with a *tabula rasa*, a clean slate, I said to myself and loaded the trunk of the car with clinking bags and cartons. Fresh snow lay on the rooftops of houses like icing on cake. I scraped the frost off the car window, coaxed the engine out of its winter slumber, and headed for the nearest bottle bank.

I entered the traffic circle and wanted to exit at the bottle bank, but when I glimpsed the lineup of other cars that had already pulled up to it, I decided to drive around a few more times. After the tenth round, I started getting dizzy. Luckily, however, there was a break in the queue, and I quickly headed for it. Pedestrians were also coming from all directions, toting bags of gleaming glass. The Swiss are big on recycling and this station was a model of its kind.

The containers were neatly separated for green, brown and white glass. There were receptacles for used batteries and old tin cans and above them all a sign proclaimed that dumping hours are from Monday to Saturday, 7.00 – 19.00.

This reminded me of a story about a high-ranking French manager, employed by a large pharmaceutical company, who came to deposit his bottles one evening at 8 pm. He was ready to toss in his first empty 3,000 franc Château Petrus when two policemen popped out from behind the containers.

They had been hiding there to catch some unsuspecting culprit. They marched the poor man off to the nearest police station where he had to pay a fine for disturbing *die Ruhe und Ordnung*, the peace and quiet. I believe he was so shaken that he gave up drinking, at least in Switzerland.

There was no danger of lurking cops on a Saturday at 11 o'clock in the morning, so I started unloading the bottles and made my way to the hole

marked "green". As I ruefully chucked in my first delicious Pommery, I wondered how the colour blind coped with the situation.

"This is *stressy*," said a man standing next to me. He was trying to stuff a magnum bottle of Dôle into the opening.

"Makes you realise how much you've been drinking," I said.

"I didn't drink it all by myself!" he answered defensively.

"Of course not. It's always the friends who booze it up."

"Happy New Year to that," he said and walked away.

As I was fishing for white bottles down at the bottom of my bag, a blond woman of about 50 appeared and shook her head.

"*Alkoholiker*," she exclaimed, "this neighbourhood is full of alcoholics!"

A shudder of guilt went through the rest of us as we furtively tried to dispose of the evidence.

"I suppose your bag is full of empty jam jars," countered an old man.

I actually did have two jam jars in my bag, along with one fizzy grape juice bottle for the only teetotaller in my circle of friends. How I cherished him at that moment.

"I'm crazy about marmalade," I said, flaunting one of the jars. "Can eat it by the ton."

I was about to leave, thinking what a rich morning it had been communicating with these usually so reticent people, when I heard my name peal through the crisp air.

"Hi, Roger," it sounded again.

Oh my God, it was someone from work!

"Hi, Mathias," I said. "What are you doing here?"

"Just bringing some bottles."

I looked at the small bag and said, "I guess you don't drink much."

"Oh, yes I do." He smiled. "But I bring the empties every day. Makes it look better."

He tossed two quarter-litre champagne bottles into the green opening and sauntered off.

Well, I guess from now on I'll be going more regularly to our friendly neighbourhood bottle bank.

Hildi's Horn

It was the hottest summer in recorded history and the usually lush Alpine meadows had begun to resemble old hairbrushes. Cows were too lethargic to swing their bells; the throats of yodellers were so parched they could emit only croaks; flag throwers fanned themselves with their flags instead of ceremoniously flipping them in the air. Due to the great water shortage, the government decreed that all alphorns be used as receptacles to catch any raindrops that might miraculously fall.

In the village of Zermatt the situation was acute. The income from tourists had dried up too. City Swiss were staying home and spending their vacations on their balconies with beer or ice tea. A 'Bollywood' film company from Mumbai stopped shooting a three-hour musical set in the Alps and went back to India because the waterfalls had disappeared. Without such a romantic backdrop how could the heroine get her sari wet and have it cling seductively to her body? Asian visitors were buying mineral water instead of watches and jewellery. Only the English seemed impervious to the heat and kept on coming to climb the Matterhorn in the midday sun.

One July night something happened to make the situation even worse. Ueli Urstein, a shopkeeper in Zermatt, woke up at precisely 3.52 am to the sound of a tremendous crash. At first he thought his wife had fallen out of the bed. But when he looked over he could see her ample bosom heaving in a beam of moonlight that had just penetrated their bedroom. Ill at ease, he slipped out from under the sheets and crept to the window of their chalet. He pushed aside the shrivelled geraniums and peered into the night. There he saw something which made the few remaining hairs on his head stand on end. All of his life he had gazed at the *Horu*, as the Matterhorn is known in the local dialect, gazed fondly at the majestic peak soaring heavenward, with its unique tilt that had made the mountain an icon and brought fame and glory to Zermatt. The sight had always filled Ueli with a sense of awe. Now it horrified him.

He rushed back to the bed and shook his wife.

"Wake up, Vrenie, wake up!"

She groaned and pushed him away, but he shook her again.

"Get up," he shouted, "get up!"

"*Um Himmelswillen*," she groaned, rubbing her eyes. "What's wrong?"

"The peak . . . the peak . . . " he could hardly bring out the words, "the Horu has . . . lost its peak!"

"Have you been drinking too much kirsch?" she said pushing him back.

"No . . . I swear . . . come to the window." He grabbed her arm and pulled her across the wooden floor. "Look."

"*Heiliger Bimban*!" she gasped. "You're right."

There in the moonlight the Matterhorn, the Pyramid of Switzerland, which had adorned chocolate wrappers for over a hundred years and was the object of countless photographs and oil paintings, stood where it had always stood, except that its peak had, well, sort of broken off. It lay at the foot of the mountain like the head of a toppled king.

Lights flashed on throughout the village; shutters banged open and heads popped out of windows. Ueli and his wife ran down to the main street where people were gathering together in their nightgowns and pyjamas.

"An earthquake!" cried a woman.

"The end of the world!" moaned a man.

"Just a natural geophysical phenomenon," said a professor from Zurich. "No cause for panic."

Ueli hurried to wake his friend, Paul Edelweiss, who almost had a heart attack when he heard the news.

"We must keep this quiet," said Paul, who was head of the tourist office," otherwise we'll be ruined."

It was of course impossible to conceal. Not since the burning of the Lucerne Chapel Bridge in 1993 had a story hit the media so fast. All the world's major newspapers stopped the presses to splash their front-pages with headlines such as, "Matterhorn Peak Plummets"; "The Fall of a Giant"; and "Swiss Icon Loses Head".

"What are we going to do?" Paul moaned to Ueli that evening when he saw the news on TV. "We're nothing without the peak."

Ueli thought for a moment and said, "Wait . . . there was a Zürcher this morning who said he knows why it happened…"

"Where is he?" Paul jumped up from the armchair. "Take me to him…instantly!"

They found the professor in a Raclette-Stübli. He was just about to pop a potato dripping with delicious golden melted cheese into his mouth when Paul and Ueli burst into the restaurant.

"Stop!" They both yelled and grabbed his arm.

The potato fell onto the professor's lap.

"What's the meaning of this?" he said curtly.

"The peak," Paul said. "You know what happened."

"Yes, but is that any reason to ruin my meal!"

Ueli Urstein apologized to the professor and told him the reason for their intrusion.

"You're our only hope," he added.

The professor felt flattered. He thought for a minute while trying to wipe away the stain on his trousers.

"Well, it's quite simple," he said. "The extreme heat has melted the permafrost, causing the upper rock strata to loosen."

"The perma . . . what?" said Ueli and Paul.

"Permafrost," the professor repeated, rubbing his trousers harder. "That's a layer of permanent ice that binds the rock together."

"So what can we do?"

"Theoretically," the professor went on, finally abandoning the stain, "the peak could be . . . how shall I put it in lay terms? Could be . . . glued on."

"Glued on!"

"Yes, theoretically, if a powerful enough adhesive were used, it would theoretically be . . . "

"Never mind all this theory," boomed Paul Edelweiss, "let's get down to facts!"

"Glue . . . what glue?" Ueli Urstein's lips stuck to the 'g'.

"I do believe an epoxy resin adhesive could do the trick." The professor smiled. "A two-part epoxy, of course."

"Of course," Paul said, "a two-part apoxy."

"Epoxy," the professor corrected. "It belongs to a category of synthetic thermosetting compounds which are widely used in industry to bond non-organic materials such as ceramic tiles, metals, and ..."

"Let's do it!" Paul Edelweiss shouted.

The next day Paul called an emergency council meeting to form a "Save the Matterhorn" Task Force, which the members unanimously voted the professor to head. Since the project required lots of funds, Zermatt made an appeal to their fellow countrymen and women. The Swiss, ever ready to support worthy causes, flocked to their local post offices to make donations per *Einzahlungschein*. The next step was to seek corporate sponsors and it didn't take long to find them. A chemical company said it would provide the epoxy resins and several construction firms volunteered cranes and manpower. The Swiss Army also promised to despatch helicopters to the scene. After a mere two weeks of hectic preparation, everything was ready.

On a Wednesday morning, the professor stood at the base camp, with Ueli Urstein and Paul Edelweiss on either side. Reporters and photographers flapped about them like pigeons. TV crews were busy setting up their cameras for a live coverage.

"Is it true," a reporter asked, shoving a microphone up to the professor's mouth, "that this is the greatest engineering feat since the construction of the pyramids?"

"Well, I would say that's an overstatement, however . . . "

Before the professor could finish his sentence, the news broke: "Matterhorn Fix Tougher than Pyramids".

The professor pressed his way through the media and climbed up onto a high platform, from which he could direct the whole operation like a conductor leading his orchestra. Scaffolding surrounded the top part of the Matterhorn where a ring of giant cranes had been erected to hoist the peak. Five helicopters hovered above the raw cleft where the peak had fallen off, ready to spray a special strong epoxy resin onto the jagged surface. This was the touchiest part of the operation because the adhesive could solidify too quickly or slowly, if the precise amount of curing agent were not added at exactly the right time.

When the professor gave a signal, dozens of pulleys began to shudder and groan. The cranes bent forward as the massive rock peak began to budge. For a moment it looked like they might buckle under the tremendous strain, but then the peak inched upwards, higher and higher until it was suspended just above the top. The professor waved and the helicopters began spraying the surface with their sticky load.

"That's a double apoxy resin compound," Paul Edelweiss explained patiently to a reporter who was interviewing him at the base camp.

Then came the most dramatic moment of the operation: fitting the peak into its original position. Poised against the azure sky, it swung slightly in the afternoon breeze.

"A little bit more to the left," the professor shouted into his cell phone. "That's it . . . gently . . . slow . . . now . . . release her!"

An estimated two billion people watched the broadcast live on television as the peak slid flush into place with a light thump and squish. Everyone cheered and eyes grew moist with emotion. Zermatt once again had its beloved Horu.

The professor became a hero and over the years the locals started calling the mountain "Hildi's Horn", in honour of Professor Dr. Dr. Rudolf Jakob Hildi, the saviour of the Matterhorn.

*   *   *   *   *

Ueli Urstein once more lay in bed and gazed through the window. A light snow had fallen earlier that night, gracing the Matterhorn with its character- istic cap. When the moon slipped out from behind a cloud, the peak, now sturdier than ever, shimmered. Next to him, his wife breathed heavily, occasionally letting out a contented little snort. Ueli's eyelids slowly closed and soon his sleep was in harmony with hers.

It was so comforting to have everything just the way it had always been.

Swiss Me

Acknowledgements

I would like to thank the following people who inspired and encouraged me: Janet Hawley, Eileen Rojo and Vanessa von Waldow, former 'Horizon' editors at Centrepoint, where I first published my columns; Peter Schibli and Peter Zweifel, Basler Zeitung 'English Corner'; Anitra Green, 'Hello Basel'; Natalie Sanfiorenzo, 'Hello Zürich'; Leslie Rijpstra; Jennifer Donati; my invaluable illustrator, Edi Barth and his wife Pascale; Andrea Bollinger; Theodor Boder; Johannes Helbling; Lawrence Desmond; Franziska Daniels-Aurousseau; Peter Gissler; Lynn Hawley; Mathias Usteri; George Imanidis; Virginia Wittmann; Marjorie Crocket; Jean-Jacques Rinnert; Karen Bergmann; Jim and Jennifer Hill-Krzys; Kathy Hartmann; Susan Kuranoff; Joel and Petra Arida; Joy Staehle; Carolyn Medley; René Taschner; Marcel Joerg, Network Relocation; Werner Rizzato; Fredy Bruder; members of my Thin Raft Writing Group: Dave and Asitta Garbutt-Tabatabai, Andrew Shields, Dan Daniels, Bridget Thomas, Andrew DeBoo, Hilary Jacobson, Catherine Matter, Christine Gerber-Rutt, Edessa Ramos, Suzanne Zweizig; and finally Dianne Dicks and Angela Joos of Bergli Books for making it all possible.

About the author

Roger Bonner, a native Swiss who can trace his ancestry back to 1585, was born in Geneva but grew up in Los Angeles, California. When he returned to Switzerland at the age of twenty-one, he suffered severe culture shock. He realised he would have to live without palm trees and also learn to speak German. Over the years, however, he has integrated so successfully that he now even dreams in Schwyzerdüütsch!

He worked for many years in the Basel pharmaceutical industry, first as translator and English teacher, then as editor and medical writer until taking early retirement.

Roger Bonner has written prize-winning poetry, short stories and articles that have been published in various American and British literary magazines. He is a regular contributor of humorous columns and stories to 'Horizon', 'Hello Basel', 'Hello

Zürich' and the Basler Zeitung's online 'English Corner'. He still lives in Basel and teaches English and has his own writing and editing business called 'Right Style'. For more information about him and his writing visit www.roger-bonner.ch.

About the illustrator

Edi Barth, an American-Swiss, was born in Seattle, Washington. He came to Switzerland with his family at the tender age of seven. After working in the music industry, he studied art and drawing with the Basler artist Lukas Wunderer before attending the 'Ecole des Beaux Arts' in Vevey. His cartoons have appeared in numerous newspapers and magazines, including 'Nebelspalter', 'Saison Küche', 'Surprise', 'Tip-Magazin' and 'Toaster'. He also designs greeting cards, posters, flyers, tattoos and company logos. He illustrated a medical book for a large pharmaceutical company and his work has been shown in many exhibitions and art fairs in Switzerland and abroad. A collection of his cartoons called *Menue Surprise* has been published in book form.

About Bergli Books

Bergli Books publishes, promotes and distributes books in English that focus on travel, on living in Switzerland and on intercultural matters:

Ticking Along with the Swiss, edited by Dianne Dicks, entertaining and informative personal experiences of many 'foreigners' living in Switzerland. ISBN 3-9520002-4-8.

Ticking Along Too, edited by Dianne Dicks, has more personal experiences, a mix of social commentary, warm admiration and observations of the Swiss as friends, neighbors and business partners. ISBN 3-9520002-1-3.

Ticking Along Free, edited by Dianne Dicks, with more stories about living with the Swiss, this time also featuring some prominent Swiss writers. ISBN 3-905252-02-3

Ticking Along on Tape, a 60-minute audio cassette with a selection of ten readings from *Ticking Along with the Swiss* and *Ticking Along Too*. ISBN 3-905252-00-7.

Cupid's Wild Arrows; *intercultural romance and its consequences*, edited by Dianne Dicks, contains personal experiences of 55 authors living with two worlds in one partnership. ISBN 3-9520002-2-1.

Laughing Along with the Swiss by Paul Bilton has everything you need to know to endear you to the Swiss forever. ISBN 3-905252-01-5.

A Taste of Switzerland, by Sue Style, with over 50 recipes that show the richness of this country's diverse gastronomic cultures. ISBN 3-9520002-7-2.

The Surprising Wines of Switzerland, *a practical guide to Switzerland's best kept secret*, by John C. Sloan, an objective and comprehensive description of Swiss wines. ISBN 3-9520002-6-4.

Inside Outlandish, by Susan Tuttle, illustrated by ANNA, a collection of essays that takes you to the heart of feeling at home in strange, new places. ISBN 3-9520002-8-0.

Berne; a portrait of Switzerland's federal capital, of its people, culture and spirit, by Peter Studer (photographs), Walter Däpp, Bernhard Giger and Peter Krebs. ISBN 3-9520002-9-9.

Red Benches and others; *a journal/notebook for your viewpoints*, with photography of benches throughout Switzerland by Clive Minnitt and Frimmel Smith and blank pages for your notes. ISBN 3-905252-08-2.

Once Upon an Alp by Eugene V. Epstein. A selection of the best stories from this well-known American/Swiss humorist ISBN 3-905252-05-8.

Lifting the Mask – *your guide to Basel Fasnacht*, by Peter Habicht, illustrations by Fredy Prack. ISBN 3-905252-04-X.

pfyffe ruesse schränze – *eine Einfühung in die Basler Fasnacht*, von Peter Habicht, Illustrationen von Fredy Prack. (German edition of *Lifting the Mask*.) ISBN 3-905252-09-0.

Beyond Chocolate – *understanding Swiss culture*, by Margaret Oertig-Davidson, an in-depth discussion of the cultural attitudes and values of the Swiss for newcomers and long-term residents. ISBN 3-905252-06-6.

Schokolade ist nicht alles – *ein Leitfaden zur Schweizer Kultur*, von Margaret Oertig-Davidson. Ein Führer durch die Schweizer Lebensart für jeden Neuankömmling und alle, die sich bereits als Insider fühlen. (German edition of *Beyond Chocolate*.) ISBN 3-905252-10-4.

Culture Smart Switzerland, by Kendall Maycock. A quick guide to customs, etiquette and history of Switzerland. ISBN 3-905252-12-0.

Hoi – your Swiss German survival guide, by Sergio J. Lievano and Nicole Egger. A colourful and lively guide to enjoy learning and speaking Swiss German. With it you can learn over 2000 words and phrases to help you feel at home. And over 200 cartoons and illustrations make learning fun and easy. ***Hoi*** includes an English to Swiss German and a Swiss German to English dictionary. ISBN 3-905252-13-9.

Also available from Bergli Books:

Living and Working in Switzerland, by David Hampshire, published by Survival Books. Contents: finding a job, permits and visas, working conditions, education, public transport, sports and much more.

Ask for a catalog or visit www.bergli.ch.

Dear Reader,

Your opinion can help us. We would like to know what you think of Swiss Me.

Where did you learn about this book?

Had you heard about Bergli Books before reading this book?

What did you enjoy about this book?

Any criticism?

Would you like to receive more information about the books we publish and distribute? If so, please give us your name and address and we'll send you a catalog.

Name

Address

City / Country

(cut out page, fold here, staple and mail to:)

Bergli Books
Rümelinsplatz 19
CH-4001 Basel
Switzerland